sally pockets

Written by: Tomme Kornegay

Illustrated by: David Furnal

WestBow Press books may be ordered through booksellers or by contacting:

WestBow Press
A Division of Thomas Nelson & Zondervan
1663 Liberty Drive
Bloomington, IN 47403
www.westbowpress.com
844.714.3454

Because of the dynamic nature of the Internet, any web addresses or links contained in this book may have changed since publication and may no longer be valid. The views expressed in this work are solely those of the author and do not necessarily reflect the views of the publisher, and the publisher hereby disclaims any responsibility for them.

Any people depicted in stock imagery provided by Getty Images are models, and such images are being used for illustrative purposes only. Certain stock imagery © Getty Images.

ISBN: 978-1-6642-0984-8 (sc)
ISBN: 978-1-6642-0986-2 (hc)
ISBN: 978-1-6642-0985-5 (e)

Library of Congress Control Number: 2020920720

Print information available on the last page.

WestBow Press rev. date: 11/17/2020

WESTBOW
P R E S S®
A DIVISION OF THOMAS NELSON
& ZONDERVAN

I dedicate this book to: God and his everlasting Grace, patience and love.

To my parents, Tom and June Kornegay. Travelling all over the world, the lessons were always the same: Be kind to others, love yourself so you can love others, be honest & straight-forward, share with others, always, always treat others the way you want to be treated and never hurt anyone on purpose.

 I watched and I learned. I listened and I learned. I loved and I learned. Thank you, Mom and Dad.

To my children, Tammy and Julia, thank you for putting up with your crazy Mother who has loved you longer than anyone, except God.

To the rest of my family, especially my brother, Pat and my Father's widow/and my friend, Suheyla. My world (and my family) also includes my friends that became family. You are my treasures here on earth. Thank you..

Thank you, again, God for all these precious blessings to my heart.

Foreword

This is my first published book, thus, no list of Authors that have reviewed Sally Pockets. I do, however have friends from throughout the United States that have read it and those reviews are listed below.

"Sally Pockets is a beloved tale that takes me back to my days of childhood, sitting on the front porch of a small home in rural Appalachia, listening to stories of my Grandmother and her children. Even though she is long gone, her homemade creations remain just like Sally Pockets and have been passed down from generation to generation. Sally Pockets is a sure to be classic that will transport its readers back to a simpler time. This is a must-read heartwarming tale."

Angela Moran, Technical Secretary, Oliver Springs, TN 37840

"Sally Pockets is an endearing story that not only captures the innocence of childhood, but also captures the beauty of a mother's love for her children. Its sure to become a classic."

5th Grade English/Language Arts (ELA) at Dyllis Springs Elementary School in Oliver Springs, Tennessee, Rebecca Sensibaugh,Harriman, TN 37748

"I LOVE your story. LOVE, LOVE, LOVE it. I especially love the use of the dialect and the glossary in the back - so clever!!!"

Katrina Longo, Paralegal, Minneapolis, Minnesota

PREFACE

In 2005, Sally Pockets came into my life in an early morning dream. In that dream, a little girl and her Mother were sitting on a fallen old tree trunk in the woods, talking to each other about the different configurations of the Acorns. (I thought that odd!! I had never before dreamed about anyone or anything I didn't know.)

I awoke sitting straight up, confused and disoriented.

Later that morning, I felt God coaxing me to the Laptop. I typed most all day, words filling the page one after another, as if I were a stream, eager to accept the snow melt from the mountains, all at one time. I have learned not to question God!

I have never forgotten that dream. It frequented my thoughts until I finally had to retrieve the typed pages in 2008. I was shocked. It was INDEED, GOD's VOICE! How could I NOT KNOW, then? Maybe I wasn't ready to receive it? I don't know. That's when I had it copywrited.

How do I know, now? Because my personal relationship with my Redeemer has become primary in my life, and there is no mistaking my Fathter's voice.

Vagely, I remember typing without questioning the words that rushed to my heart. I read it outloud to myself and was immediately comforted by the presence of the Holy Spirit.

Another 12 years, and here we are. This time God told me exactly what to do. He said, clear as a bell, **"My child, it is time. We cannot wait a moment longer. Tell them to love one another. All my children need to be reminded they are loved. Take it throughout the world."**

sallyPOCKETS

Hello and Welcome!

Today, your heart is embarking on a journey that will change you. This is a story about family, & at times, the hardships, and sacrifices that many families encounter and experience; all seen through the eyes of a bright little 9-year-old Arkansas girl from the mountains.

If you have family, then welcome to your extended family. If you do not, we welcome you into ours. We are always here for you because God is always here for us. All of us! Yes, my friend, even you! We live in love, acceptance, patience, and kindness. We are not perfect, but we are perfect for each other, as you will soon see.

We're just 'a wait'n fer ya'all to come and sit with us "fer a spell."

My name is Chloe. I was the oldest child in a family of seven (including Mr. Foot).

Let me introduce you!

We are the Ledbetters. We lived in the Ozark Mountains of Arkansas in the 1930's.

Pa - (Isiah) Pa was a quiet man, 'a walk'n with his shoulders straight and proud; a man of few words, but one look from them blue eyes of his'n was our quiet assurance that we were safe, loved and protected. Even though he never said "I love you," we always knew that he did.

Pa did not take to strong drink or using profanity. He toiled away in them dirty old coal mines from early morn'n to just before "dark o'clock." He came home, chopped wood for the fire, took a puff or two off his pipe; and with a smile and a wink, sat himself down at the table to give thanks to the Lord for all our blessin's. (Ma was the bestest cook in whole world.) With nothing but gravy left on that old plate of his'n, he'd "sop that up" with a biscuit and another wink. 'Bout then he'd announce, "I'm 'a gonna sit for a spell."

Push'n away from the table, he would take a few steps over to his rock'n chair, settle his tired, old self in, and smile as he bragged about his coon dog, Mr. Foot (named "Foot" because when Mr. Foot was 'a grow'n, he was always 'a stepp'n on Pa's foot).

Pa would light up that pipe of his'n, take one final puff, and 'a start 'a snor'in. That was the way he ended his days. We knew we'd not see them blue eyes of his'n till supper the next night.

Ma - (Sally) Every morn'n before we young'uns "raised up," Ma would walk over to the window and fix her eyes on that old tree of her'n. I knew, even then, that Ma and her thoughts were somewhere none of us were invited. She seemed to be at peace, while 'a peer'n through the broken pane of glass. Every time she was 'a stare'n at that tree, she'd start 'a giggle'n like our little Mary. What was that secret of hers that made her eyes light up so?

You know what? I think that was the best gift God ever gave me – Ma! Ma and me, we were "bestest friends." I miss that sweet Ma of mine.

I' 'a seen pictures of Ma when she was a young'n. She was sooooo "purdy," so thin that you had to "a look twice to see her once," and with that long black hair of her'n just "a shine'n and blow'n in the breeze." No wonder Pa was sweet on her.

Ma was not well. But her touch...always the same, as warm, and soft as a puppy dog's ear.

Grammy - Grammy had small twinkl'n eyes and a smile that 'a made your insides jump up and down. She spent the days in that rock'n chair of hers that 'a sang us to sleep with its familiar squeaks 'a mak'n sweet music with the floor. She was a mite crippled but took great pride in shuffl'n around the table every day. When she and Ma were sitt'n together, you could hardly tell them apart – except for Ma's eyes. They were sad and dark. Ma always looked like she was 'a go'n to cry.

Chloe (me) - I am a 9-year-old country girl with thick, red hair, controlled only with pigtails. I had (as Ma used to say) tiny "laughing freckles" 'a rest'n on my nose. I'm 'a think'n I was a typical little girl – a stinker of a "tomboy," a little "sassy" at times, but always tender and soft-spoken with Ma and Grammy; always patient and kind with my Dougie, Matthew, Mary and Pa.

(Mr. Foot can wear you plumb out – he can wear your patience "plumb out." That four-legged old coon dog would 'a howl at 'nuth'n and shake them floppy ears of his 'til the 'flapp'n sound drove you plumb silly. Then he'd look 'atcha with those sad old eyes of his'n and turn your heart into "mush".......silly old dog!)

"Dougers," (Dougie) was my 8-year-old brother and friend; hair as white as a cloud and 'a point'in straight up at the sun. They called him a tow-head **What is that?** That boy was stubborn......would not even comb that stuff or "give it a wash'n!"

Dougie was a "critter "chas'n, bug eat'n" , little boy. He 'a pestered his brothers and sisters with anything he knew would make them squeal. We loved being together. Dougers and I, even if it was just 'a digg'n worms, 'a fish'n, a' trapp'n rabbits for dinner, or playing pranks on each other.

My little brother could turn into a "Doug" that always made Ma's eyes twinkle like them there light'n bugs. Doug was as "sweet as bucket o'candy" around her. What a smile she had when she was 'a feel'n good. All he had to do for a smile was to make that "squirrely, cock-eyed" face of his, and dance like a "silly old donkey after 'a finish'n his oats!"

Matthew, my little 5-year-old brother, was a "follower," a sweet tempered, one dimpled, "little bit of a fella." He carried a book, "My Friend, Freddie" with him, no matter where he went. He could not read; but knew it all by heart after a passel of "hunker'n down sessions on the porch" with Grammy. That book was his trusted "hide'n place," and constant companion.

Mary, my 4-year-old sister, "peanut butter dimples" 'a look'n atcha with every smile; loud, "full of mischief attitude, unpredictable, uncontrollable, but ever so sweet when she wanted somth'n. She'd look up atcha with them big, round eyes of her'n and smile like an angel.

She was a charmer, that one, but could "turn on a dime" and pull a prank on anyone faster than you could say, Mary! She loved 'a eat'n bugs, worms, or whatever happened to live in the "clean dirt," as she called it.

Home was a ramshackle log cabin with a much loved sitt'n porch right there, just 'a look'n at 'ya say'n, "Come on in. Ya'll want some coffee." We had a one room cabin (which was common for "country folk" in the 1930's) that was impossible for Ma to keep clean, but that Ma of ours managed to tidy up, sweep the dirt from the floor and wash them dishes every single night (with a little help from her oldest daughter, Chloe.)

Our fireplace was (bigger than all of us standing elbow to elbow) for 'a cook'n and 'a warm'n. We gathered 'round a long wooden plank table (that Pa made) with two long benches to use for homework, when not eat'n a meal; a tiny kitchen in the corner, beds hidden behind Grammy's hanging quilts, and most importantly, a "sitt'n place" for all the family to share the happens' of the day with each other. That's right! It was all in that cozy one room cabin.

Ma and Pa, went from year to year wearing their same old, faded cover'ns. The children never heard them complain about what they had or did not have. They were just Ma and Pa, grateful for the old shoes that had been patched, overalls that were still patched "over a patch," but warm and comfy, and dresses that were well made for a life of purpose by Ma. Such were the days and life in the Ozark mountains of Arkansas.

Even though much of September had come and gone, Chloe's birthday was today. She was 10 years old. She crossed her fingers, closed her eyes said a silent prayer for that red ribbon she had her heart 'a set on.

Our cabin survived only by the Grace of God and a whole lot of pray'n. It leaked and often whistled a sorry tune from the wind and rain, but thankfully the old tree 'a sitt'n next to the hill took every beat'n we had from the that "nasty weather". Burrrrr, it was cold (cold as a frog 'a hopp'n after his breakfast in the snow.)

Thank God, because he put that old cabin next to the aptly named, Abundance Hill (named for bunch 'o them berry patches scattered about for Ma's 'á mak'n them sweet pies of her'n.) It held our "home" up for many years. Had it not been for that hill, the cabin would 'a fallen! You know what? We were blessed to have a home. We were blessed to have family. Everything we had and shared was a blessing.

"Ya'll, Come on in and sit 'a spell! We got the coffee on fer ya."

Children, remember to be thankful for what you do have, instead of what you do not have!

Chloe's dress made a soft swishing sound as she skipped down the forest path toward home. It was a trip she made daily to and from school. She was familiar with its sounds, its smells, and the soft carpet of pine needles that crunched beneath her feet. It was always a peaceful, happy walk home.

This day, her stride was noticeably longer and faster, 'cuz she was 'a fix'n to get "the 'purdest thing she'd ever seen." It was her birthday and her Ma had a special present for her.

Chloe was a dutiful child, and when at home, shadowed her Ma's every move. This sweet, unassuming little girl did not think there was anything in the world more wonderful than being a Ma. Her Ma made the best Blueberry and Gooseberry pies in the "Holler." Her bread was "yummy good," and she knew the best medicine for an "owie." (We had a lot of those). And Miss Chloe wanted to be just like her!

Chloe didn't like 'a wear'n dresses and could hardly wait to take them off when she got home. Overalls were her favorite things to wear. Her brother, Dougie, was bigger than she was, even though he was younger. His Overalls always had just the right amount of "give" to 'em. She did have to cinch have to cinch them up with a rope around the waist to keep from tripping over her own two feet, though.

Every September the children waited for their new garments (to keep them from "showing their private ever-thang's). They were 'a hope'n to get new'uns made by "Ma," and maybe, a pair of shoes, (usually passed down from one to the other), but new to them. Money was scarce. They didn't 'a see many new cover'ns back then. Maybe this would be this would be the year for a new shirt for Dougie, and dresses for the girls. Old or new, everyone was maybe a little disappointed, but grateful for being able to share each other's "already broken in" cover'ns from the year before. "Oh, them clothes of our'n seen a lot of miles," said Chloe. Ma knitted socks for everyone, so socks were a "no nevermind."

This day was special for Chloe. She reached the edge of the forest and could clearly see her home edge of the forest and could clearly see her home. Running her little heart out, she finally reached the porch steps. Out of breath, she collapsed, happy to see her Ma waiting for her. Ma was 'a lean'n against the front door with her arms behind her back. Sally waited for her Ma to say something!

Several months prior to this day, Sally and her Ma went on their weekly hunt for Acorns Greens, and firewood. (Ma would grind the meat of the Acorns to make flour for all her bake'n), The Greens and firewood were quickly gathered and loaded into their hand wagon.

Those tasks done, they excitedly "fixed their eyes" on that Oak tree ahead. Pull'n the wagon near, they sat themselves down on a fallen tree trunk, little critters 'a scatter'n everywhere. How content they were, Ma and Chloe. This was their favorite part; together, just the two of them.

For an hour or so, they talked and laughed as they chose only the best Acorns to bring home. Often, they would find one that seemed to "tickle their 'inerds," and make them giggle. (It was "their secret game".) They gave the Acorns names (Acorns that Ma did not use) and brought the special one's home to keep for "a spell."

Time and again, the two of them would find one that seemed to have its own personality. It was a race to see who could come up with just the right name. The most interesting Acorns were toted home and kept for a while, pretend'n, and 'a give'n them their own little stories.

On the most recent Acorn hunt, they both picked up the same Acorn and squealed with the glee of young children as they realized it had a face – a face that looked like Ma. For a moment they stared at each other, and then the Acorn. They would most certainly have to keep this one. Ma threw it in one of her pockets and they sang, "Jesus Loves Me" all the way home.

Chloe could not forget that face. She wanted to look at it forever. She often slipped it out of Ma's pocket when Ma wasn't 'a lookin and "do a little pretend'n on her own."

"Ma, what you got 'a hide'n" behind your back? Is that my present, Ma?" Ma looked down at her and said, "land 'o sakes , Missy, I plumb forgot it was your birthday." Ma waited 'til Chloe's mouth started pucker'in up, then slowly extended her arm and handed Chloe her gift.

Chloe, Sally, and the Magic Acorn

The smile on her Ma's face was almost like Grammy's. Chloe carefully opened what she knew would be "the most wonderful treasure of her life."

Still breathless, Chloe shook with anticipation as she reached into the bag to grab 'a hold of this surprise of hers. "A red ribbon," she thought. "What a wonderful surprise. She could wear it to school tomorrow and be the envy of all the girls." (Living in the mountains presented little opportunity for a young girl to acquire such a fetching prize.)

"Mmmm-m-m-m-m," she said to herself, as she felt inside the bag. "This ain't no ribbon." Her little hand still probing inside the bag touched something that felt like nothing she had ever touched before. While holding onto the bag tightly with one hand, she pulled it out, carefully with the other.

In disbelief, she held it to her heart, looked up at her Ma, looked at "it" again." looked at her Ma again, and moved "it" to her freckled little cheek in an attempt to grasp its meaning. Her tears made their way down her face to rest, finally on the collar of her dress. Chloe had never, ever seen or held anything so beautiful.

Looking at this most precious of gifts, she remembers that several days ago, she noticed one of the Ma's pockets was missing. "How odd," she thought, "I'll have to ask Ma about that after I get finished braiding Mary's hair.

There it was - right in front of her. She wasn't 'a believe'n her eyes.

What do you suppose her gift was? Can you guess?

In her hand, she held a tiny doll that Ma had made for Chloe. Her dress was Ma's very own pocket. The doll's head was the wonderful acorn they had found together – it looked just like her Ma The arms, hands and legs were crocheted.

Still shedding tears of joy, Chloe looked up at her Ma with such adoration, and was so full of emotion, she couldn't speak.. Her Ma leaned down, put that gentle hand of hers on Chloe's shoulder and asked her, "Are you 'a like'n it, sweetheart?" Chloe rose, still holding the doll to her heart, and hugged her Ma so hard that she could feel her Ma's bones.

"Ma, this doll is the sweetest, most "purdiest,' most special gift in all the world. No one will ever have a doll as 'purdy and loved as this. Ma, I love you so much! Is it mine to keep for ever and ever? Can I have it till I die, Ma? Can I, Ma?" Ma gave her one of those 'a waited for "Ma hugs" and said, "Chloe, honey, I been 'a work'n on her every night fer ya."

Ma asked Chloe what she was going to name her new doll. Without taking a breath, Chloe said, "Ma, I'm going to name her after you, of course, Sally."

From that day on, Chloe would not wear 'a cover'n unless it had pockets, so that she could carry Sally Pockets with her always. (Chloe would spend her lifetime not 'a wear'n any cover'ns that did not have pockets for her precious "Sally.")

Ma (Sally) was ill when she made "Sally Pockets" for Chloe. Struggle as she did, Ma went to heaven three years later at the age of 35. Chloe's world, as she knew it, stopped.

Chloe took Ma's place as much as a 13-year-old could; cooked, cleaned, made sure she got an education and all her siblings got theirs, as well. Pa and Chloe worked together for 20 years before God called her Pa to Heaven.

Chloe grew up to be a lovely young lady, married and had five children of her own. She was happy and well, with those children, 8 grandchildren, and 3 great Grandchildren. She spent 50 years of her life as a doctor searching for the cure to her Ma's disease. Chloe never found it, but she always felt Ma near, and knows God was taking good care of her and Pa.

Chloe was 86 years old and still carried "Sally" with her. Sally is a little tattered and worn, but there she was – in Chloe's pocket every day of her life.

Chloe and her little four-legged companion, Miss Foot (her cat of 15 years) lived together in town, nestled in their sweet home surrounded by their cherished forest of wonders. After having lost her husband to a heart attack 5 years 'a fore, Miss Foot was a real bless'n to have.

Sitt'n on the porch swing, waiting for her cornbread to bake and her children and grandchildren to arrive, she took a deep sigh, leaned her head back on the porch swing, and allowed her mind to wander back to the Holler when all her family was in one place.

Chloe realized her journey in life was abundant with sweet memories of yesteryear; love, family and "Sally Pockets." How did Ma know that Sally Pockets would accompany Chloe on all her journeys throughout life? How did Ma know Chloe had the strength and courage to succeed and prosper? Well, it turns out, Ma's are pretty smart.

Ma and Pa are both in Heaven now. Dougie, Matthew and Mary are in different parts of the county with their own families. Mr. Foot (God rest his soul) went to heaven five years after Ma passed. The family get-togethers came every five years, way too far apart for Chloe.

Oh, there goes the buzzer, rudely interrupting her "walk back in time." Her cornbread was ready. As she took the cornbread from the oven, she heard horns 'a honk'n – the kids were there, all of them. Yippee!!

And, you know what? Sally Pockets still went everywhere with Miss Chloe. I am sure that Sally even went with Chloe to heaven when God called her home.

From the moment Ma handed "Sally Pockets" to Chloe, "Sally" lived in every single pocket Chloe wore. Chloe was a little old then, but the love her Ma put into that doll would last forever. Life goes on, but this part of Chloe's story has paused for now. She will share more stories with you throughout the years.

"Thank you for letting us share our family with you.
Ya'll come back now, 'ya hear! You are family!"

Remember, a gift from your heart is the greatest gift of all. Why? Because it comes from **your heart, and you must always <u>share</u> your heart with others**. Never give your heart away, though. Why? Because your love has a home in your very own heart. God lives in your heart. If you give one away, the other will be lonely. They must always be together.

Studying the Ozark dialect is like looking back into the past of the English language. The "purity" that the Ozarkers retained was that of **Elizabethan English**.

A **dialect** called Ozark English is spoken in the Ozark Mountain region of northwestern Arkansas and southeastern Missouri. It is a close relative of the Scotch-Irish dialect spoken in the Appalachian Mountains, as many settlers migrated from Appalachia to Arkansas beginning in the late 1830s. Scholarship posits that the geographic location and subsequent isolation of the Ozark Mountains allowed for the preservation of select archaic properties of the dialect spoken by Appalachian settlers. This isolation fostered an independent development of the dialect that set Ozark English apart from what is widely considered standard American English. Like its Appalachian cousin, Ozark English is commonly linked to stereotypes that depict the mountain culture as backward and uneducated.

Ozark English was studied throughout the 1900s, but scholars largely relied on limited and anecdotal data. More recent scholarship such as that performed by Dube and her team does not dismiss the validity of these records. The goal is to assert the Elizabethan influences that exist in isolated communities within the region while acknowledging the changes that are occurring in the speech of younger Ozarkers. Ozark English—once nurtured by the region's geographic location and its isolation from outside influence—has today become a fusion of the old and new, a unique dialect born of a people's cultural history.

For additional information:
Brooks, Blevins. *Hill Folks: A History of Arkansas Ozarkers and Their image* Chapel Hill: University of North Carolina Press, 2002.

DEFINITIONS OF THE LEDBETTERS LANGUAGE AS TOLD BY CHLOE: (in alphabetical order).

'a cookin and 'a warm'n – cooking and warming

'a grow'n – growing

'a looki'n at 'ya say'n -looking at you and welcoming you into their home

'a mak'n – making

'a make'n – making

'a peer'n – looking at tree of hers

'a shin'n and blow'n – shinning and blowing

'a show'n their private everthangs – showing everything

'a stepp'n on Pa's foot – stepping

'a walk'n with his shoulders – walking with his shoulders

'a wear'n – wearing

Blessin's – blessings

'bout - about

    'cuz she was 'a fix'n to – because she was going to'our'n – ours

    'til – until

    Atcha – at you

    Clean dirt – dirt that you had to dig down to....it wasn't clean, but Mary thought it was.

    Cover'ns - clothes

    Critter-chas'n, bug-eaten, chasing animals, bugs, and always 'a look'n for trouble .

    Dark o'clock – Sunset

His'n, he'd – his, he would

Holler -a small valley

I 'a seen – I have seen

I'm gonna sit for a spell – I'm going to sit down for a while

Light'n bugs – Lightening bugs

No nevermind – don't worry about it.

Plumb out – wear out your patience

Purdy, purdiest – pretty

R'aised up – got out of bed

Sassy – bold and a little feisty

Sop it up – gather the gravy with his biscuit

Towhead – light blonde or white hair

Us'n – us

Ya'll come join us and sit a spell! We got the coffee on fer 'ya – Please come sit down for a while. – You all come in. We'll rest a little and share coffee with you

About the Author

Tomme was born in Tucson, Arizona in 1944. She was raised all over the world by an Air Force family in the comforting arms of two wonderdful people, Tom and June Kornegay.

She changed her name after her dear Father passed away of Heart disease in 1986. His name was Thomas Daniel Kornegay. Hers was Lynda June Kornegay. Theirs was a typical "Daddy's little girl" relationship throughout life. So, she changed hers to Tomme (for Tom & me) Daniela Kornegay. It's who she always has been and who she always will be.

She traveled the world for 20 years with her family (two brothers, mom, dad and usually a Boxer dog.) - every two and a half years, another state or another country. She and her younger brother, Pat, reunited twenty years ago and have become as close as "Macaroni and Cheese."

Tomme has two daughters, Tammy and Julia, both living their dreams on opposite ends of the country. Get-togethers are sadly, few and far between.

Tomme has been writing heartfelt poems, prose, and stories for 35 years. Every single one of them was God's gift to her "that just keeps on giving."

She now lives in and loves Colorado.

She asked God into her heart in 1980. HIS presence has been constant and "lived" every day of her life. God changes you? Yes, HE does. She's thankful for every moment of every day of her life for HIS patience, HIS trust, their convenent, and most of all for making her a better,God loving person. She doesn't preach, but will share HIM with you, if you ask. This woman lives what she believes.

Her latest gift from HIM is Sally Pockets. It came to her in the wee hours of the morning. When she sat down to put it on paper, she knew it was HIS latest gift to her, but told her to give it to others. This is what she has done. Welcome to the world of Sally Pockets.

Lightning Source UK Ltd.
Milton Keynes UK
UKHW020741031220
374507UK00002B/90